For Leah Nicole Fitzgerald, a beautiful little Buddha.
With special love to my teachers Adrian Feldmann
and Wendy Finster – H.M.

For Sue – J.V.

Julie Vivas used watercolor for the illustrations in this book.

Kane/Miller Book Publishers, Inc.
First American Edition 2007
by Kane/Miller Book Publishers, Inc.
La Jolla, California

Originally published in Australia in 2006
by Working Title Press, Kingswood, SA

Text copyright © Helen Manos 2006
Illustrations copyright © Julie Vivas 2006

Library of Congress Control Number: 2007921054
Printed and bound in China
1 2 3 4 5 6 7 8 9 10

ISBN: 978-1-933605-51-7

SAMSARA
DOG

Written by Helen Manos
Illustrated by Julie Vivas

Kane/Miller
BOOK PUBLISHERS

For we are all travelers on the wheel of life.

We halt, we pause and take new births.

Take comfort, then, you beings wandering in weary Samsara,

And hear in every footfall the sound of blissful compassion.

For compassion is the tree that shelters all beings.

It is the universal bridge

That dispels the misty ignorance of the world

And leads the weary traveler out of Samsara into Nirvana.

Adapted from the 8th-century writings of Shantideva

Samsara Dog lived many lives. Some of his lives were very long, some lasted only a few days. Dog never remembered them. But sometimes the sound of low chanting flitted across his memory and puzzled him for a moment.

Coming back again and again was how it was meant to be. Dog lived each life as it came until, finally, he learned the most important lesson of all.

In one of his lives Dog lived on the street. It stank of old men in old coats, and tomcats with whiskers stiff as swords.

Dog ruled the street. He sniffed the tracks of the cunning cats. He sorted out the other dogs, baring his broken teeth in their faces until they ran off, howling.

Sometimes, when the moon stared down and the street was quiet, one of the old men would call, "Dog, get over here, will you?"

But Dog would slit his melon-colored eyes and turn away.

Dog loved nobody. Dog trusted nobody. Dog lived for himself.

One night, stretched out on an old sack, Dog felt more weary than he'd ever felt before. He closed his eyes and drifted peacefully away.

Dog came back to live
with a biker gang that
smelled of animal skins
and grease.

The bikers brawled
with other gangs. Dog
tore around, snapping and
growling at their heels.
When he was with the
pack, he could smell
danger. Dog loved danger.
It made his blood run hot.

The bikers chased each
other up and down roads,
looking for trouble.

Riding on the front of
the bike, with the wind
screaming in his teeth, Dog
howled his joy out loud.

One night the wail of
a siren sliced through the
darkness. The bikers sped up.
Roads and trees blurred. The
bike swerved and reared up
like a wild thing. Dog felt
himself fly through the air.
As he went, he howled at
the wide night sky.

He came back as a sniffer dog.

He sniffed his way along airport corridors and inside kitchens where rats scratched behind greasy walls. He sniffed boots, skin and belly-crunching fear. Fear was the worst. It thrashed inside him like a trapped bird. It made him want to bite.

"You're so wild," his trainer said. "Come here, Dog."

But Dog turned his back. Dog loved nobody. Dog lived for himself.

Dog worked until the day he died. As he floated off, he felt his trainer's warm hand stroking him on his way.

Dog was born very small and very sick.

His tiny eyes never opened. He heard low chanting and a gentle voice say, "Sometimes life is a terrible struggle, little dog. Sometimes we only manage to arrive before we have to move on again."

Dog tried to hold on, but the thin thread of this life was fast unraveling.

"Don't be afraid. Coming back again and again is how it must be," said the gentle voice. "When it is time, you will know great love. Go and learn what you must learn."

And the sound of the chanting carried him off.

Dog shared his next life with a street juggler.

Day after day the juggler stood on the street and tossed balls like long colored loops into the sky. Sometimes they slipped through his fingers and rolled away. Then no one gave him money, and he and Dog went hungry.

One damp afternoon, as the juggler sent the balls flying high into the air, Dog jumped and caught each one in his mouth. People stopped to watch. Dog turned and danced in dizzy circles.

The crowd laughed. Someone dropped coins on the ground.

That night the juggler wrapped his arms around him and sighed, "I'm glad you're here, Dog."

People came from all around to see Dog. His dizzy dance made everyone smile.

One day Dog lay on his blanket, too tired to move. The juggler held him in his arms and cried as his friend slipped away.

He came back as a rescue dog on a cold, craggy mountain.

When avalanches crashed down the mountain, the dog rescue team sniffed through icy layers, looking for survivors. Each time they found someone, the other dogs were praised and kissed.

But Dog's owner never praised him. He spent most of his time skiing in the mountains.

Left alone, Dog watched and waited. All around him vast slopes fell away like frosty waterfalls. The low hum of the alpine wind carried snatches of old songs and distant memories.

A heaviness crept inside Dog. He had never felt like this, not in all his lives. He opened his mouth and cried, and the sound tumbled off the lonely mountainside.

One night Dog felt a familiar stiffness in his bones, and whimpered.

"Poor dog," his owner said as he knelt beside him. "You've worked long and hard, and I've never thanked you."

He put his arms around Dog and kissed him on the nose.

And with his last breath, Dog kissed him back.

Dog moved through a tunnel of light into his next
life, to a big house with four girls who adored him.

They dressed him in sunglasses, tiaras and
feather boas, and stuck stars in his hair.

They fought to sit next to him and to have him
sleep on their beds.

They took him to ballet classes and taught him
to do pirouettes.

When the smallest Sugar Plum Fairy fell sick with chickenpox, Dog took her place, and everyone laughed.

Dog ate cream puffs, golden fudge and chocolate whenever he wanted. His hips grew stiff and his stomach grew round.

On the night Dog lay dying, the four girls held him and sobbed.

Dog was born in a boat shed. His first memory was of someone singing. He crawled off to find the sound.

And Dog found the boy.

The boy sneaked Dog into his bedroom. He gave him a biscuit. "I'm going to keep you, but you'll have to learn to eat everything. Mom says we can't afford a pet."

Dog settled beside a fuzzy bear that smelled of the boy's good smells.

The boy was fast. He threw himself down sandhills. He tore through creamy waves that washed back on themselves. He hummed through the days like a kite.

And tripping beside him, like a small, clumsy shadow, was Dog.

"You're my best friend," the boy said, and Dog's heart galloped with happiness.

At night they squashed together under a blanket. The boy read stories until his eyes closed and his head tipped sideways.

Curled up like two spoons, Dog and the boy caught each other's dreams.

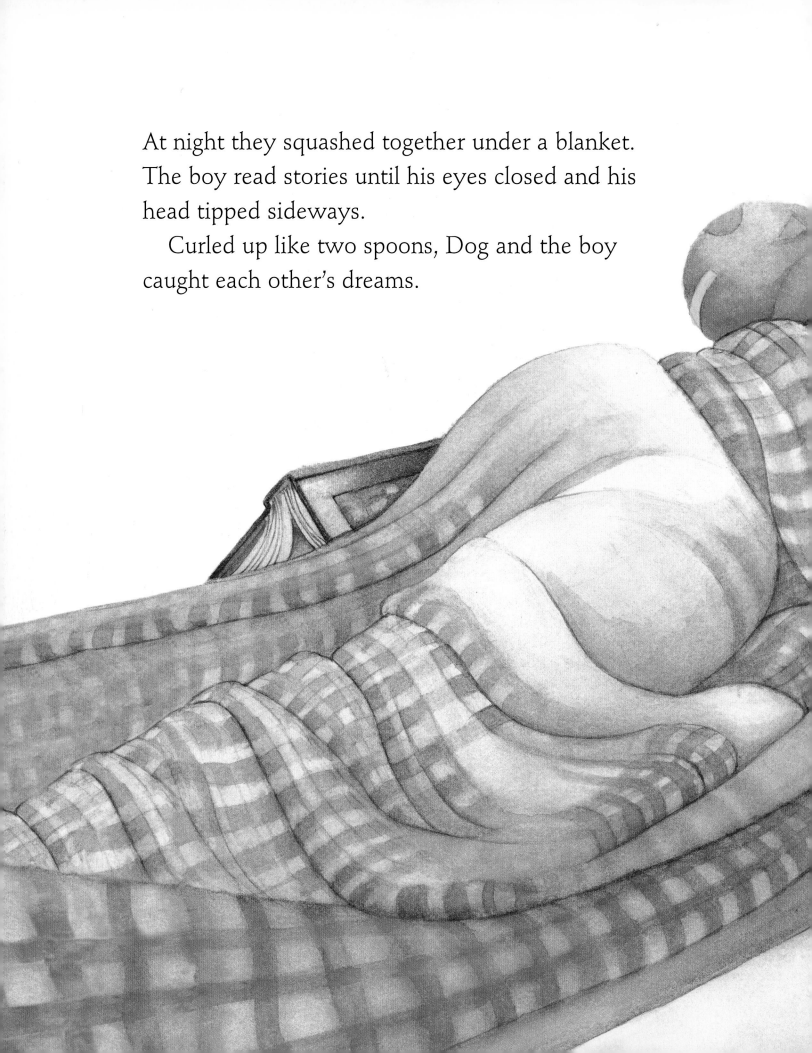

Dog grew strong. Soon he could run down the sandhills and swim through the creamy waves.

One afternoon, when Dog was chasing a tribe of gulls, the boy flung himself off a sandhill and crashed to the beach below. Dog licked the sand off his eyes and tried to help him up. But the boy didn't move.

When the first star appeared, people came and carried the boy away.

Days and nights passed. The sharp smell of fear hung around the house.

The boy's skin tasted like cold sand. Dog never took his eyes off him. And one day the boy opened his eyes and called, "My dog, where's my dog?"

"My boy's come back," sobbed his mother.

But Dog cried sad little cries because he knew not all of the boy had come back.

His eyes were as milky as jellyfish.

Dog took charge. The boy didn't *need* his eyes to see. He could *sniff* his way around. Look! Sniff here, Dog sang throatily. *This* is where wild cats have trod! *This* is where gulls with rusty feet have rested! The boy laughed and held Dog's strong neck.

Dog led the boy along the sand. He stayed with him all the long summer days, guiding him through the waves and then bumping him back to shore.

At night the boy told Dog stories about pirates and sailing ships and mermaids.

When he was with the boy, Dog's heart skimmed like a song. He loved the boy more than he loved himself.

The boy grew up. He wrote stories and read bits of them aloud. Dog lay by the fire and listened. Sometimes, when the stories didn't go well, the boy threw the pages on the floor. Dog chewed them up and made him laugh.

Years passed. Dog hardly ever went outside now. Nothing was better than being with the boy.

One evening, as Dog came to the end of his life, the boy slipped his arms around his neck.

"There's something I have to tell you," he said.

"Once there was a dog that lived many lives. He came to live with a small boy. When there were only dark clouds in the boy's life, his dog gave him hope. When the boy was lost and afraid, his dog gave him comfort and the gift of great love."

Dog looked lovingly into the boy's blurred face.

A deep calm settled inside him. His heart filled with trust and joy.

Wrapped in the boy's arms, Dog felt himself grow lighter and lighter.

And he never came back again.

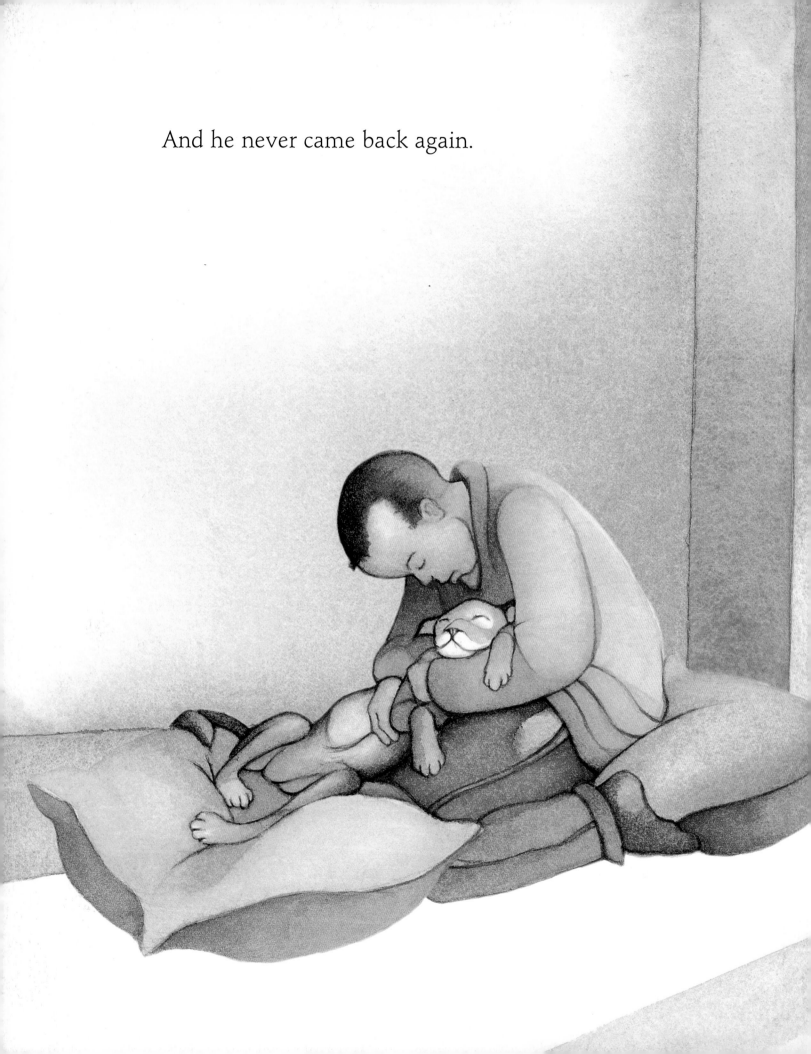